# Vorg World

# For Matthew
# and Jacob Atkins

Find out more about **Ricky Rocket** at
**www.shoo-rayner.co.uk**

ORCHARD BOOKS
338 Euston Road, London NW1 3BH
*Orchard Books Australia*
Hachette Children's Books
Level 17/207 Kent St, Sydney, NSW 2000

ISBN 1 84616 035 9 (hardback)
ISBN 1 84616 390 0 (paperback)

First published in Great Britain in 2006
First paperback publication in 2007

Text and illustrations © Shoo Rayner 2006

The right of Shoo Rayner to be identified as the author and illustrator of this work has
been asserted by him in accordance with the Copyright, Designs and Patents Act, 1988.
A CIP catalogue record for this book is available from the British Library.

1 3 5 7 9 10 8 6 4 2 (hardback)
1 3 5 7 9 10 8 6 4 2 (paperback)

Printed in Great Britain

# Ricky Rocket

## Vorg World

# Shoo Rayner

ORCHARD BOOKS

Ricky Rocket and his best friend,
**Bubbles,** had been fans of the Evil
Lord Vorg since they were tiny.

Mum had brought them and Ricky's
little sister, Sue, to Vorg World, the
most exciting theme park on the
planet of Hammerhead.

"Oh wow!" Ricky nudged Bubbles. "Look over there...there's a Rogon Squid! They're the best fighter pilots in the universe! What's he doing in Vorg World?"

"No one's a better pilot than the Evil Lord Vorg!" Bubbles said.

"Well...duh!" Ricky waved his hand in front of Bubbles' face to see if his brain was still connected. "Evil Lord Vorg is a teevee programme – this is real life...remember?"

The Rogon Squid was running away from a teevee crew who were trying to give him something. When the crew saw Ricky, Bubbles and Sue, they gave up the chase and came towards them.

"Hello!" said their leader. "We're giving away samples of Super Nova, a fantastic new treat that ruins your teeth and appetite at the same time! Would you like to try some? We'd like to film your reactions for the teevee."

Super Nova was a ball of green, fluffy stuff on a stick. Ricky, Bubbles and Sue tore off huge chunks and stuffed them in their mouths.

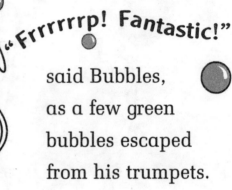

"Frrrrrrp! Fantastic!"

said Bubbles, as a few green bubbles escaped from his trumpets.

"Oogly, woogly-umptious,"

said Sue, in her irritating girly way.

## "Blldbllntbob!"

Ricky spluttered with a full mouth. "Hey, there's a joke on the stick. What do spacemen play on long journeys?"

"That's an old one," said Bubbles. "Astro-noughts and crosses!"

The teevee crew thanked them and went off to find someone else to film.

A Martian visited the sun and didn't burn up.
He went at night!

How do you send a baby astronaut to sleep?
You ROCK-ET!

9

Ricky rubbed his hands together. "Right! Time to go on the rides."

"Wooo-hoo!" They ran off looking for the biggest, scariest ride they could find.

# SUPER NOVA SWEETS

**Super Nova**®
is made from the
**Callisto Cabbage**
that grows in the
stinkbogs on the
moon of Callisto.

The **Callisto Cabbages**
are boiled for
three days.
They are then
mashed and put
on a stick to dry.

The best part of **Super Nova**®
are the jokes that are printed
on the sticks. A few favourites:

> Why did the human become an astronaut?
> Because he was no earthly good!

> Where do you leave your spaceship?
> At a parking meteor!

> Why was the astronaut hungry?
> Because it was LAUNCH-time!

**They screeched to a halt.** They stood with their eyes and mouths wide open and gasped. "A-ma-zing!"

A giant, multicoloured sign flashed:

THE LORD VORG
BATTLE ARENA

A small fleet of fighter ships zoomed through the air in the arena, blasting their space canons. They were all trying to destroy the Evil Lord Vorg's battle cruiser.

"Look!" Ricky pointed at a pair of
tiny fighters that had been shot down
by Lord Vorg. "They're spinning out
of control! They're going to crash!"

"That was amazing!" whooped
Bubbles. "Did you see the way they
both pulled up at the last second
and made soft landings?"

None of the little fighters were
a match for the Master of the Skies.
The Evil Lord Vorg was invincible.

# LORD VORG AND HIS BATTLESHIP

*Lord Vorg's Helmet*

**Lord Vorg** has been thrilling young teevee viewers for years. His daring flying skills can be seen each weekday afternoon on the **Lord Vorg Show.**

**Lord Vorg** has never been defeated in battle. His ship is armed with high-powered lasers and an armoured layer of **Likton** skin. It is powered by three JBL twelve-megawatt light motors.

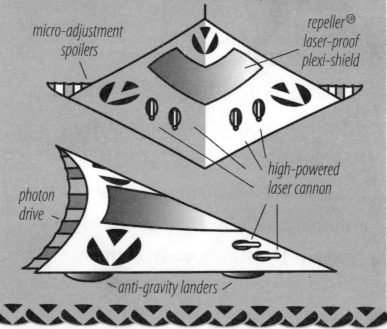

*micro-adjustment spoilers*

*repeller® laser-proof plexi-shield*

*high-powered laser cannon*

*photon drive*

*anti-gravity landers*

**"We have got to go on that!"** Ricky said. "It looks in-cred-i-ble!"

"No way!" Mum said. "It looks really dangerous!"

"It's perfectly safe, madam," said the ticket collector. "The whole of Vorg World is run by P.A.N.T.S.S. The Perfect Accident Neutralization Total Safety System. Everything is computer controlled. Nothing can go wrong."

"I'm sorry," Mum insisted. She turned to Ricky and Bubbles. "There is no way I'm going to let you two fly around and be shot at by that horrid Lord Vorg!"

Just then, the huge hulk of Lord Vorg's menacing battle cruiser flew over and hovered over them. The Evil Lord himself gazed out of the cockpit. Ricky's heart thumped like the tail of an Andovian Kandaboo.

# ANDOVIAN KANDABOO

**Andovian Kandaboo** have very strong tails, which they beat against the ground, turning the mud into a gloopy soup.

**Kandaboo** carry their young in a pouch on their backs. When the **babies** poke their heads out they say,

**"Kanda - boo!"**

**Gloop frogs** live in the millions of muddy pools that cover Andovia.

Lord Vorg's eyes bored into him like laser beams. "You've got to let me have a go, Mum!" Ricky pleaded. "He's challenging me. I can shoot him down, I know I can!"

"No!" Mum was firm.

Lord Vorg threw back his head and laughed his hideous laugh. Then he flew away to taunt someone else.

**Mum only let Ricky and Bubbles** go on rides that Sue liked. They went on the dismal Vortex of Venus

and the wretched Wobbling Wheel of Woo.

On the pathetic, whirling Teacups of Doom, Sue filled the air with the kind of ear-splitting, blood-curdling, brain-jamming scream that little Earth girls are famous for all over the universe.

"I'm not going on another ride with her!" Ricky insisted. "My ears can't take any more!" He was determined to go on a proper, exciting ride. He looked around and pointed at the Magno Bouncer.

"I'm going on that!" he announced. "Come on, Bubbles."

Sue whimpered. "I don't like it, it's too scary."

"And it's much too dangerous," said Mum.

"Oh come on, Mum," Ricky begged. "We haven't had a go on anything good yet. It's all controlled by P.A.N.T.S.S. Nothing can go wrong...please can we? ...please...pretty please?"

Ricky batted his eyelids and looked angelic.

Mum was too tired to argue. "Oh, all right then," she sighed. "But don't blame me if you're sick!"

As they waited in line, Ricky and
Bubbles watched as all sorts of
creatures, wearing special magno
harnesses, bounced around on the
magnetic waves.

26

Soon, wearing their tight-fitting harnesses and magno boots, they walked onto the floor of the Magno Bouncer. Ricky shouted over the pounding music. "Hey look at the smoke on the floor. You can't see your feet!"

A siren wailed.
Lights blazed.
"Here we go!"
yelled Bubbles.
Ricky felt
himself being
lifted off the floor.
It was like being
on a trampoline,
except that there
wasn't anything
solid to bounce
on, just an
invisible,
magnetic force.

"Hey, look at me!" Ricky shouted, as he bounced off the wall.

Ricky and Bubbles hurled themselves at each other. They bounced apart, the same way that two magnets repel each other. No matter how they tumbled or turned, their magno boots always got them the right way up again. It was brilliant!

Bubbles shrieked with laughter and
a thin stream of orange bubbles trailed
from his trumpets. He stopped in
mid-air, and blushed. "Ooops! I do
beg your pardon!" Then he laughed
even more hysterically, and blew
even bigger bubbles.

Ricky felt something pulse beneath him. "Hey! What's happening?" he cried as he rose into the air. Up and up he went, until he came to a halt, suspended in mid-air, high above the park.

Far below, park attendants ran around in a panic. Something had gone wrong. Ricky was stuck on a freak spike of magnetic force.

"DO NOT PANIC!" a metallic voice called. "STAY ABSOLUTELY STILL. EVERYTHING IS UNDER CONTROL. WE WILL SOON HAVE YOU BACK SAFE AND SOUND!"

Ricky looked down. A large crowd had formed. 'Oh no!" He said to himself. "That teevee crew are pointing their camera at me – how embarrassing is that? And…oh no! Mum's hysterical!"

A fire engine pushed through the crowd and raised a ladder towards him, but the magnetic effect bounced the ladder away. There was no escape!

"I'm going to be here for ever!" Ricky told himself as he revolved slowly in the air.

"HOLD ON!" called the metallic voice again. "WE'RE TRYING SOMETHING ELSE…DON'T PANIC!"

Ricky heard the whining engine of a fighter ship from the Lord Vorg Battle Arena. The small craft cruised over him and a hatch opened in its belly.

A robot arm grabbed him and pulled Ricky to safety. The crowd cheered.

He was almost safely inside the ship when a huge, blue, crackling spark zapped Ricky's magno harness. The robot arm sprang open and let go!

KRA-A-ACK!

Ricky felt
strangely calm.
He heard an
ear-splitting,
blood-curdling,
brain-jamming
scream from
the crowd
down below.

"Ahh!" Ricky
thought. "That
sounds like my
dear sister, Sue!"

As Ricky hurtled towards the ground,
his life flashed before his eyes. "Oh
look!" Ricky thought. "There's Lord
Vorg's battle cruiser swooping down
towards me...I wonder why?"

The last thing Ricky remembered was a long, thin tendril that shot out of a hatch and wrapped itself around his body.

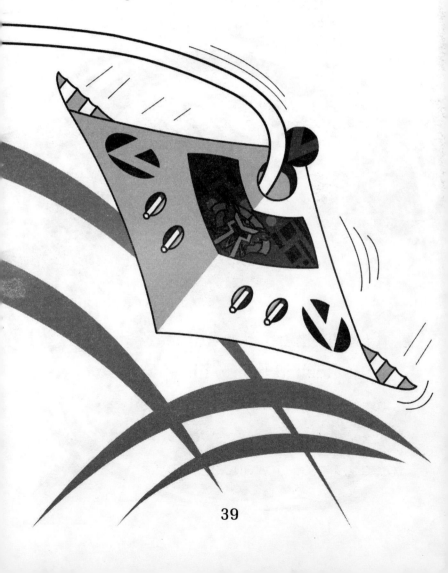

**Ricky felt he had dreamed** this dream before. He was staring into the red, glowing eyes of the Evil Lord Vorg! He was doomed. Nothing could save him now!

Then, suddenly, the Evil One's head slipped off! It was a mask, and beneath it was the Rogon Squid he had seen earlier in the day.

Ricky shook his head. "That's not how my dream goes!"

"No dream!" the Rogon Squid said, matter-of-factly. "Caught you before you fall."

"Ah!" gasped Ricky, who had already forgotten that he'd nearly fallen to his death. "That's why no one could shoot you down. Everyone knows that Rogon Squid are the best fighter pilots in the universe.

The Squid smiled and explained. "I disguise as Lord Vorg. Fly at Vorg World for fun. You tell everyone it really Lord Vorg what save you. Don't want friends to know I do job like this at weekend... I be big joke, ha ha!"

# ROGON SQUID

**Rogon Squid** have three brains, one each for up, down and sideways.

Their brains are perfectly tuned to the **Standard Space Vertical** so they always know which way they are going. This is what makes them such great pilots.

Cross section of a Rogon Squid brain.

The teevee crew filmed Ricky as he and Lord Vorg emerged from the battle cruiser together. The crowd cheered as they interviewed Ricky for the six o'clock news.

"I thought Lord Vorg was going to blast me out of the sky!" Ricky trilled into the camera.

"Actually," Ricky gave Lord Vorg a friendly punch on the arm, "Lord Vorg is really quite a cool guy – once you get to know him personally."

Lord Vorg put his arm around Ricky and looked menacing for the cameras.

The park people were very sorry.
They told mum they could all
come back anytime they liked for
free – P.A.N.T.S.S. would never let
another accident happen again.

"P.A.N.T.S.S.!?" Mum shouted. "Do you really think we'd come back here again? This whole place is PANTS. That's P. A. N. T. S. – Perilous And Not Terribly Safe!"